# polly pocket™

Written by Justine Fontes
Illustrated by MADA Design, Inc.

TO: MY PEEPS
SUBJECT: EMERGENCY LEMON PARTY!!
Hi, Pals!!:P
The 411 on the weather is
gloomy again! :( But let's have a
fantabulous sunny saturday anyway! :D
Meet @ the mansion @ 2pm.
Bring every happy, sunny, lemon
yellow thing u can find.
sunshine rulez! -ttfn

Meredith® Books
Des Moines, Iowa

Shani read the note and squealed, “Fabulicious! Count on Polly to perk up even a dull day. And I so totally have the perfect props for this party!”

**Help Shani find:**

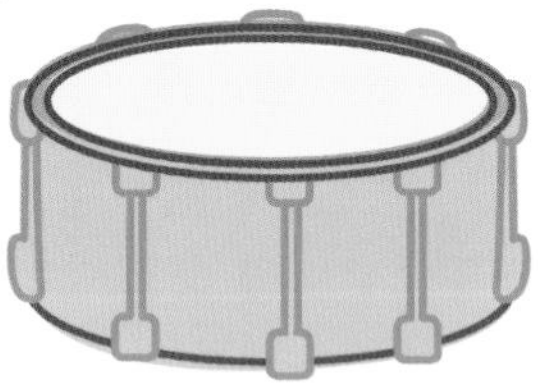

snare drum

drumsticks

maracas

bath duckie

bongo drum

duckie slippers

CD

THR
skool notes
Lemon Tree & other hits!

# FINISH

Lea was stoked too. "Polly copes with the rainy day mopes!" She looked around her room. "I have lots of yellow things and some yellow felt!!"

**Help Lea find:**

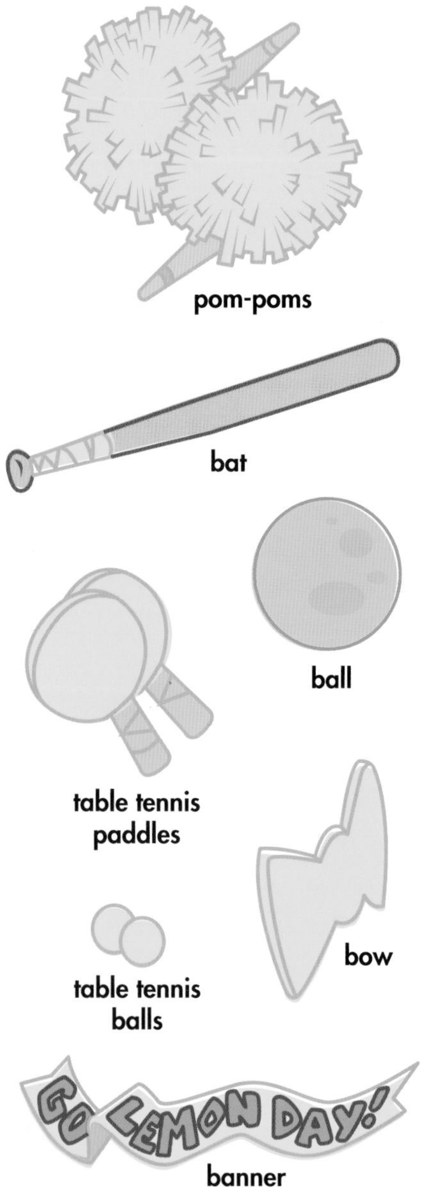

GO TEAM

Laundry gave Rick his Lemon Party inspiration. "I'll stuff my family's yellow clothes with newspaper and take a yellow scarecrow to the party. I can call him Sunny."

**Help Rick find:**

- sweatshirt
- work gloves
- sweatpants
- sneakers
- baseball hat
- socks
- rubber kickball

12

Lila typed back to Polly, "Thanks for inviting me to the ultimate rainy day party. Better bounce! My mind is spinning with yellow bling-bling and other things to bring."

**Help Lila find:**

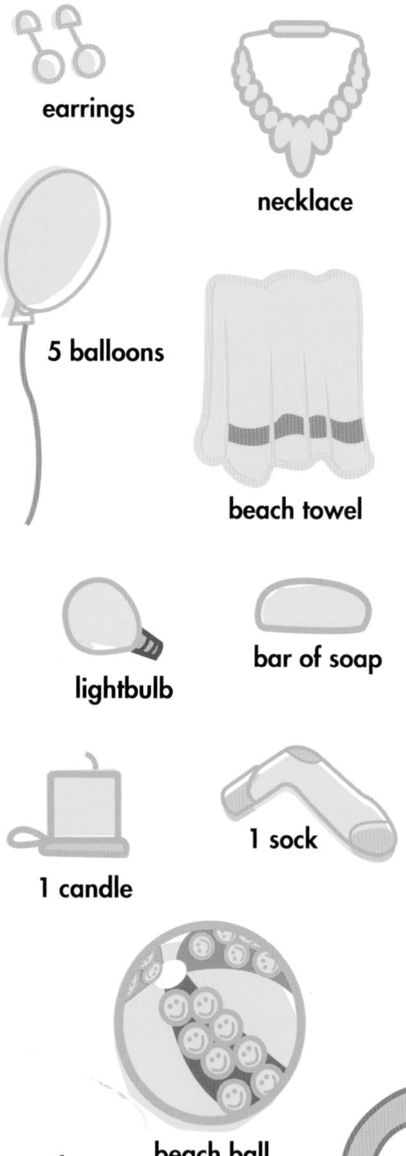

- earrings
- necklace
- 5 balloons
- beach towel
- lightbulb
- bar of soap
- 1 candle
- 1 sock
- beach ball

Crissy grooved on the Lemon Party idea too. After replying to Polly, Crissy bounced down to her kitchen to look for happy, sunny, yellow, lemon things.

**Help Crissy find:**

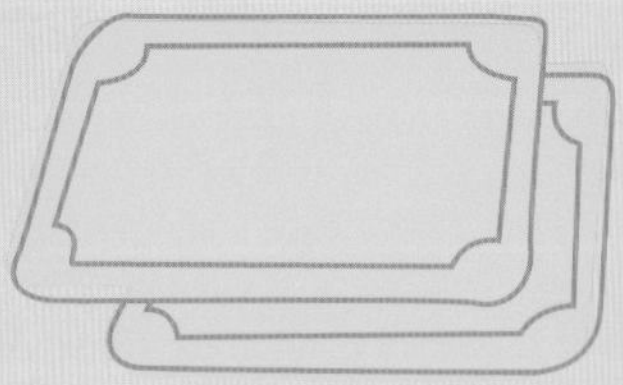

place mats

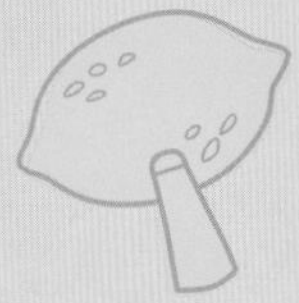

paper fan

box of gelatin

bag of popcorn

napkin rings

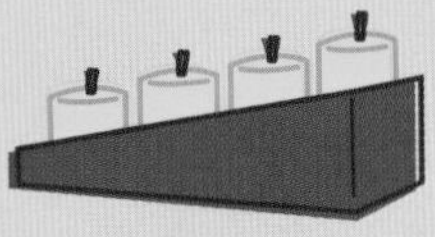

candles

big bowl

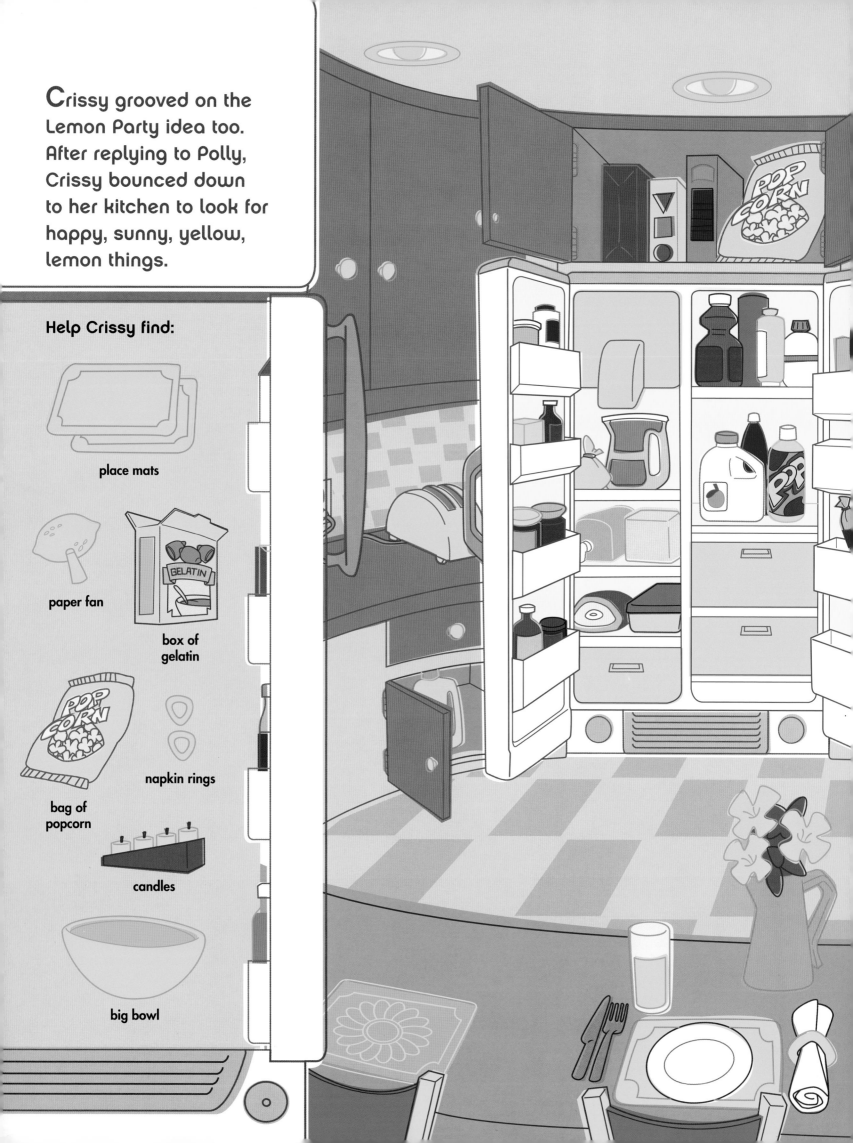

GELATIN

Todd wished he could bring his Super Lemon Ade sign to Polly's party. Then he realized, "Snap! I can photograph the sign—and lots of other yellow things!"

**Help Todd find:**

SUPER LEMON ADE
N. OAKS ST.
LEMON AVE.

When Polly's butler, Samuel, saw Polly glowing with sunny enthusiasm, he caught Lemon Party fever. He hurried to the party store for yellow everything!

**Help Samuel find:**

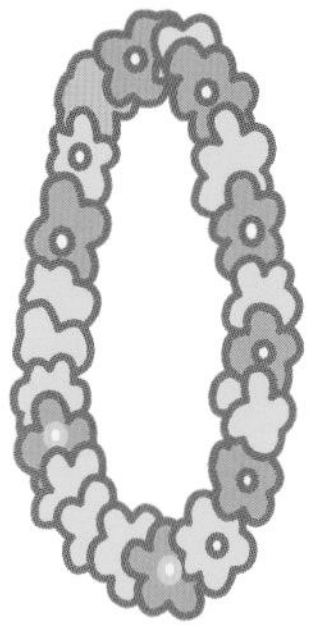

plastic flower necklaces

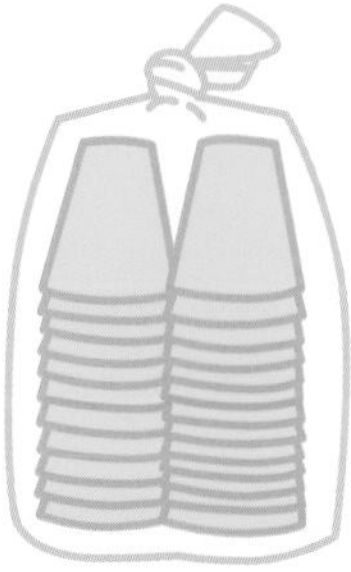

cups

forks

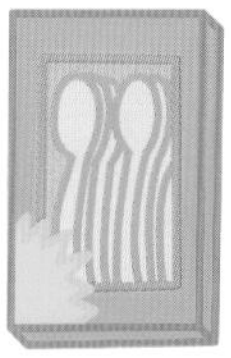

spoons

crepe paper

plates

tablecloth

party hat

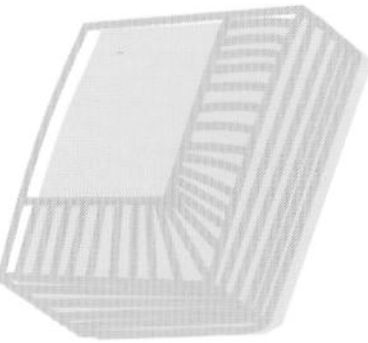

napkins

CENTRAL
4
BALLOONS
BALLOONS

The cook caught Lemon Party fever too. "Lemon meringue pie, lemon bars, and lots of other yummy yellow things to eat. This will be Polly's prettiest party yet!"

**Help the cook find:**

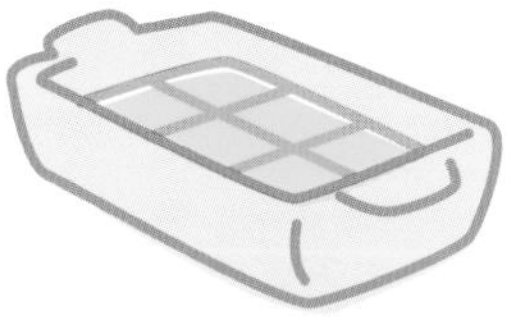

lemon bars

bananas

frozen treats

lemonade

fresh lemons

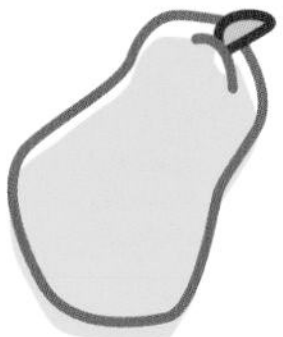

squash

yellow pepper

lemon wedges

lemon meringue pie

WHEAT
BARS

Lila's message made Polly smile. "I need to dress in yellow from head to toe!" Polly searched her dresser and closet. "Sweet! I have yellow every-thing—except shoes."

**Help Polly find:**

- vest
- hat
- knee-high socks
- scarf
- hair scrunchie
- bracelet
- sweater
- skirt

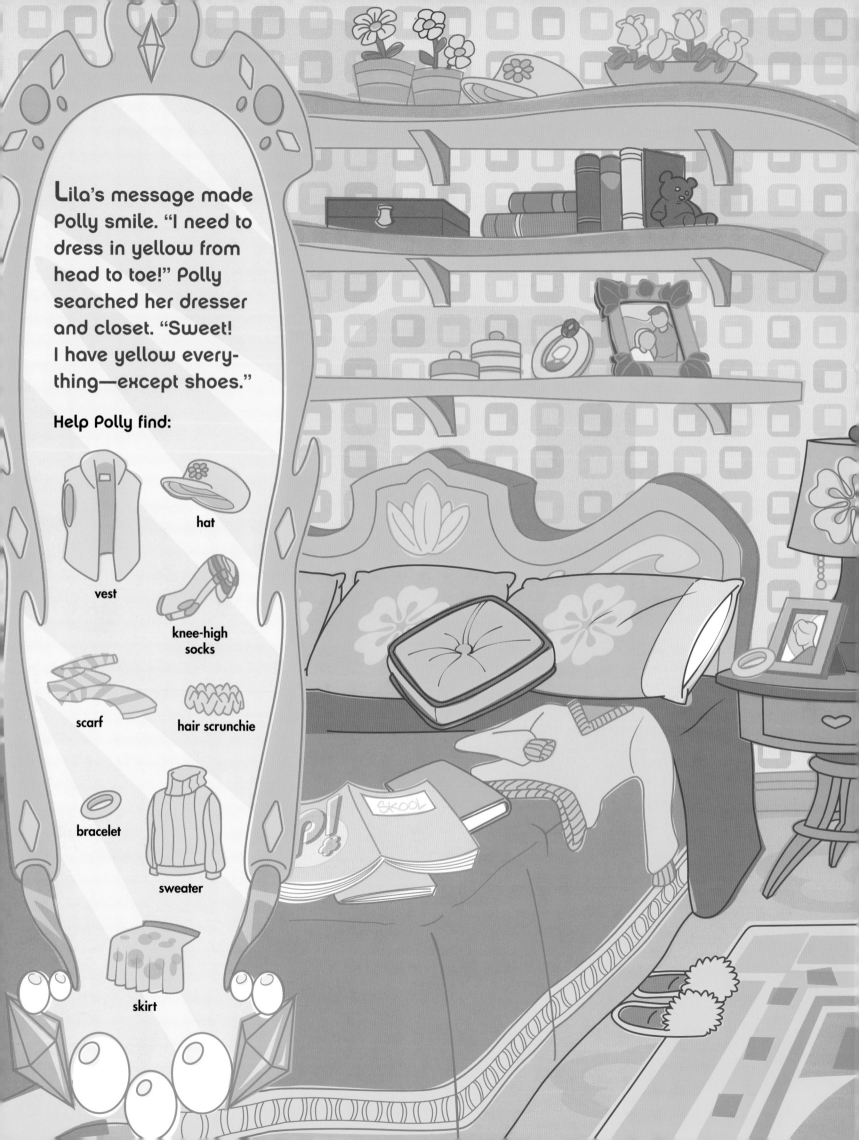

Thanks to a tip from Samuel, Polly's father found out about the Lemon Party in time to ship a box. Polly opened it, and exclaimed, "Yellow shoes!"

**Help Polly find all the goodies from her father:**

- topaz ring
- bag of lemon drops
- roses
- hat
- boots
- lamp
- pencil
- sunglasses